VOYAGE TO BRAVERY

I Am Strong

I Am Brave

I Am Powerful

JEREMIAH SHELTON

ARTIST :
SARAH HAMEED

Summary: Sam is a young boy dealing with health issues that make him feel powerless and weak until he discovers the magical land of Aurora that is filled with magical characters and charms that bolster his inner strength. Sam learns the power of support, self-love, and bravery. The powerful story takes the reader along on Sam's journey to uncover the truth and power that lies inside every child, no matter what obstacle they face.

ISBN: 978-1-64953-106-3

Book design by Jeremiah Shelton
Cover design by Jeremiah Shelton and Sarah Hameed
Illustration design by Jeremiah Shelton and Sarah Hameed
Illustration creation by Sarah Hameed

Absolute Author Publishing House

HOW TO USE YOUR POWER CAPE AND POWER POUCH DURING YOUR VOYAGE

Acorn: The Acorn was given to Sam by Goodwin. In life, we are all acorns with the potential to become a mighty oak tree. We make choices every day that decide what kind of oak we will grow into. An acorn may be small but inside is enough potential to grow an entire forest of powerful oak trees. There is so much potential in you! Your acorn is your reminder that although you may be small now, but inside of you lies the potential to not only become a mighty oak, but to grow an entire forest of trees. You are Powerful and have incredible potential, just as your Acorn does. As you hold it in your hand Repeat these words, **"I AM STRONG, I AM POWERFUL AND I AM BRAVE!"**

Mehler Anchor: Earl handed the Anchor to Sam and Told him, "This anchor represents strength. It is strong enough to hold your boat in place during the biggest storms with the mightiest of waves. More importantly, it is meant to give you strength in your darkest times, or when you are scared." When you are scared, remember this anchor will hold you steady even in the roughest storm. Hold it tight and repeat these words, **"I AM BRAVE!"**

Belief Stone (purple stone): The belief stone was given to Sam by Sarge. Sam used it to control the wind but more importantly to Believe that he could! When you start to doubt yourself take out your belief stone and repeat these words, **"I BELIEVE!"**

Promise Stone (Green Stone): The queen delivers the promise stone to Sam, as a reminder to always stay true to your word and your promises. You will make the promise to yourself to be strong, brave, and powerful and your promise stone is there to remind you that nothing can come in between you and that promise. It takes a lot of bravery to keep these promises you make to yourself. Whenever you have doubt Hold the stone in your hand and repeat the words **"I AM STRONG!"**

Power Cape: Now that you know how to use all your Power Pouch tokens, you are now officially a member of Sam's Army! You have been awarded this cape to wear anytime you need the army behind you! When you are facing something scary put on your cape and repeat, **"I AM STRONG, I AM POWERFUL, I AM BRAVE AND I BELIEVE!"** Always remember you have an Army behind you, and You will never fight alone!

To order another Book, Power Cape, Power Pouch, or to donate a book to a children's hospital, please visit:

www.voyagetobravery.com

TABLE OF CONTENTS

Definition of Superhero
: a fictional hero having extraordinary or superhuman powers
: a very heroic person

Definition of Hero
: a mythological or legendary figure often of divine descent endowed with great strength or ability
: a person who, in the opinion of others, is bold, brave, or altruistic
: a person admired for achievements and noble qualities
: one who shows great courage

Definition of Courage
: mental or moral strength to venture, persevere, and withstand danger, fear, or difficulty

Definition of Bravery
: the quality or state of having or showing mental or moral strength to face danger, fear, or difficulty

Definition of Belief
: a state or habit of mind in which trust or confidence is placed in some person or thing

Definition of Promise
: a declaration that one will do or refrain from doing something specified
: ground for expectation of success, improvement, or excellence

In the real world, true superheroes are the ones who have the biggest struggles in life. The true superhero makes a promise to themselves to fight and make this world a better place. The true superheroes live in the hearts of small children fighting huge battles. Turn the page to begin your voyage!!

CHAPTER 1

THE DOCTOR

"Mom, can we go home now?" asks Sam.

"We are almost done, sweetheart," Mom says. "As soon as the doctor sees us, we will be able to leave."

"Okay, Mom. I just want to go home. I want to be a normal kid who doesn't have to deal with this."

"I understand. We will keep fighting, and we will win this battle. You have to have faith and believe that you will get better," says Mom.

Sam looks at his mom, and his eyes start to well up with tears. He lowers his head and cries. His mother reaches over and gives Sam a huge hug. Just then, they hear a knock at the door. The doctor enters the room.

"Great news, Sam! You just finished your last treatment, and you will be able to go home now. When you get home, please take it easy and rest," says the doctor with a huge smile on his face.

Sam's mother has a huge smile on her face, but Sam has his false smile on. He is happy to go home, but he doesn't want to live in his bedroom. He wants to go outside and play. He wants to be a normal kid.

"Mom, will Dad be home when we get there?" asks Sam.

Yes, Sam. Your father is home with your sisters. He is so happy that you are coming home—he misses you!"

"I miss him too. Do you think he'll want to play football with me, or jump on the trampoline when I get home?"

"Your father would love to do those things, but you aren't allowed to go outside and play yet. You need to get rest when you get home."

"All I do is rest, Mom! I want to be a normal kid and go outside and play," exclaims Sam.

"Sam, you are so much more than a normal kid. You are the best kid that I know... You have a bigger heart than anyone I know, Sam. You are anything but 'normal.' You are special and you have a purpose in this world. Normal is boring. You are meant to do great things. Sam, I love you."

"I love you too, Mom."

Sam sits in silence, not believing what his mom just said. Purpose? "What purpose," he wonders. "Is my purpose to sleep? To lie in bed? To go to doctor appointments? What did she mean by 'purpose'?"

Mom switches the turn signal on to go into their neighborhood.

CHAPTER 2

HOME AGAIN

As their car turns down their street, Sam and his mom see a giant banner in the yard that said "Welcome Home!" There must be over a hundred balloons in the yard and on the house. Sam's eyes light up, and he temporarily forgets about his illness.

"Mom?" exclaims Sam.

"Yes, Sam?"

"Look what Dad did to our house!" he says with a smile on his face.

"Ha ha. Your father is excited to have you home—you know how he is!"

Sam has flashbacks of what the house looked like at Christmas. There are lights everywhere during the holidays. Just then, they pull into the driveway, and Sam sees his dad and two sisters holding balloons with huge smiles on their faces. Before the car is even stopped, Sam's dad opens the car door and pulls him out, gives him the biggest, longest hug he has ever had. When Sam's dad finally puts him down, his two sisters basically tackle him to the ground because they are so happy to see him. Sam dusts himself off, and they all go inside.

"Sam, look at this giant cake that we got for you! It is orange mandarin. I know it's your favorite!" says Dad lovingly, but with a hint of sadness.

"That's my favorite! I can't wait to eat a piece—and I love all the decorations!" Sam says with his face aglow.

The house has more balloons on the inside than on the outside. There are streamers hanging from the ceiling and a few presents on the table. Sam immediately runs to the kitchen table to see his cards and presents.

Sam says, "Dad, can I open my presents now?"

"Yes, Sam. I will cut everyone a piece of cake, and then we will open presents."

Everyone sits down at the table, and Sam starts to open his cards.

"Dad, where did all of these cards come from?" Sam asks. "There must be at least a hundred cards here!"

"Some are from your sisters, some are from kids at your school, and some are from a local running team that wants to show their support," Dad says with gratitude and inspiration.

Sam is overwhelmed at others taking the time to do this. He is elated by the love he feels through this gesture.

"This is amazing! So many people could care enough to do this."

Sam, you are a special kid, and they wanted to show you that you are special," says Dad.

Mom says, "See, Sam? You are not normal. You're special."

"Yes, very special," Dad agrees. "Why don't you open the presents that you have?"

Sam opens a present. Inside is a huge banner with his name on it, with hundreds of signatures. A note explains the signatures are from people who ran a dedication run in his honor because he is a special kid.

Sam is blown away and cannot understand why all these strangers would dedicate a run to him.

There is another package. Sam opens it and discovers a blanket with the running team's logo and the words "No one fights alone" embroidered on it. There is a note attached to it that reads: "Sam, we will fight with you. We can't wait to meet you. See you soon!"

"Who are these people?" Sam asks.

"People who care and who make a difference," Sam's mom answers.

"So they found a purpose, I guess," Sam remarks.

"Yes, they did, and you will find yours," Mom replies.

Sam took one look at his cake and felt sick. For a moment, he had forgotten he was sick—until his stomach reminds him.

"Sorry, guys, I don't feel good and need to lie down," Sam says.

"Sure, let us tuck you in," Mom says. She and Dad feel defeated but happy that Sam is home.

"Good night, Sam," says Mom.

"Good night, Mom. Can Charlotte sleep with me tonight?"

"Of course," Mom replies. "Charlotte! Come here, girl."

Sam hears Charlotte run up the stairs. As soon as she gets into his room, she jumps on the bed and licks Sam's face.

"Charlotte is the best dog ever. I missed her!" Sam comments to his parents. Mom and Dad give Sam a good night kiss and leave the room.

"Charlotte, you are the best dog, and I missed you," Sam says. "I wish I felt better so I could take you out to play. Mom keeps telling me that I am special and I need to find my purpose in life. I wish I knew what she meant, and I wish I knew what my purpose was."

Just then, the wind blows the window open. The room fills with the cool night's breeze that smells of lavender. Sam thinks this is odd because they have no lavender plants in their yard. He gets up and closes the window and goes to bed.

CHAPTER 3

GODWIN & THE ACORN

As the sun rises, Charlotte lifts her head.

Bark! Bark! Bark!

Charlotte is barking at Sam's bedroom window. Because Sam keeps finding his window open, he assumes it is broken. He approaches his window to close it and sees a large group of people on the running trail behind his house. There are over a hundred people out there! A lady is standing on a picnic table with a megaphone. Sam is about to shut the window, but the window will not close. He pulls with all his strength, but it will not budge. The lady with the megaphone speaks.

"Hello, everyone! My name is Christine."

Sam is taken aback because he realizes this is the group of runners who sent him the many cards and the blanket. "What are the odds of this?" Sam thinks. He listens to what she has to say.

"Thank you all for coming out to run for those who can't. Today is a dedication run. We are running for three warriors today. This team makes a difference every day in our community. Our purpose is to make the world a better place, to fight illnesses that affect our community, and to show true kindness to this world. We are much more than a running team. We are 'the change' we want to see. We are positive, and we will win. This is our 'WHY,' and this is our purpose," Christine says with conviction. "When you run today, run for those who can't! Let's go!"

Sam watches as one hundred people begin to run down the path.

Sam continues to watch all the runners finish their run. He gets inspired to run but understands if he asks his mom if he can go outside, she will tell him he cannot. Sam lowers his head and feels sorry for himself.

Just then, Sam hears a crash in his closet. He opens the door to find a shoebox had fallen from the top shelf. He opens the box and finds a pair of his old running shoes.

"I don't need any more signs, Charlotte. I am going for a run today!" Sam says.

Sam gets dressed, dusts off his old shoes, and laces them up. He waits for his parents to go into the living room so he can sneak through the kitchen and out the side door. He slowly sneaks down the stairs. Every time the stairs creak, he freezes because he doesn't want to get caught. Sam is determined to run, and today is his day. He makes it to the side door and slowly opens it. As soon as he steps outside, the smell of lavender fills his nose. The sun gently warms his skin, and he knows there is something special about the day. He has no idea of what is about to happen. His journey is about to begin.

Sam makes it to the trail and starts his run. He feels fantastic. He has no worries, and his mind is clear. For the first time in a long time, he feels like a normal kid. It is a beautiful day, and the trail runs next to a beautiful stream. With every step Sam takes, he gets himself back—but then it hits him.

About a quarter of the way through the trail, Sam wheezes with a feeling of fire in his lungs. He continues to push himself even though it is hard. He makes it through about a hundred yards farther down the path, then he suddenly feels a stabbing pain in his ribs. As much as he wants to continue, his body will not allow it.

Sam stops running, falls to his knees, and breaks out in tears. He looks up at the sky and screams, "Why can't I just be normal? I want to be able to play. Why am I like this?" With his face in his hands, he falls to the pavement, crying. Suddenly, the wind picks up, and the familiar smell of lavender fills his nose again. Big black clouds quickly form in the sky above him, blocking out the sun. He has seen nothing like this before; however, he is eerily calm. When he lowers his head, he sees a giant figure in the distance walking toward him.

Sam stands up and brushes himself off as he watches the figure get closer. He rubs his eyes in disbelief at what he is seeing. From his viewpoint, this figure seems over ten feet tall. It gets closer and closer and closer until Sam can get a clear view of it. It is an enormous "man" with long red hair, wearing a helmet with two horns sticking out from it. This is the biggest "person" Sam has ever seen; however, Sam feels safe and calm.

The mysterious figure stops right in front of Sam and looks at him with his giant blue eyes and says, "Hello, Sam. I have been waiting for you. My name is Goodwin."

"You have been waiting for me?" Sam asks.

"Yes, I have been waiting a long time for you to show up," answers Goodwin.

"Why me?" a puzzled but curious Sam asks.

Goodwin replies, "Because you are special. You are the only one who can save my world."

"Your world?" Sam asks, puzzled.

"Yes," Goodwin answers with a loud tone. "The Land of Aurora."

"What is the Land of Aurora?" Sam asks curiously.

"Let me show you..."

At that moment, Goodwin reaches into his coat pocket and pulls something out, asking Sam, "Do you know what this is?"

Sam looks at what Goodwin is holding. It appears to be an acorn. So, he answers honestly, "It's just an acorn."

"Ha ha ha. Just an acorn? Look closer. It is much more than a mere acorn. What I hold in my hand is the future. This tiny acorn has the potential to become a giant oak. Everyone you know is just like this acorn. They all start very small and grow up."

Sam, feeling very confused, replies, "Okay, it's a seed that will grow into a tree."

Goodwin looks at Sam with an enormous grin and laughs again. "It does grow into a tree, but that is not what I mean. Look at it again, and tell me what you see."

Sam examines the specimen and still sees an ordinary acorn. "I see an acorn," says Sam, slightly annoyed.

"In life, we are all acorns with the potential to become a mighty oak tree. We make choices every day that decide what kind of oak we will grow into. There is so much potential in you. Have you found your purpose yet, Sam?"

Sam thinks for a moment. There is that word, again—purpose.

"I don't know what my purpose is. I just want to be normal," Sam says.

Goodwin takes a hard stare at Sam. The clouds behind him grow dark and roll toward him. Sam is frozen by the changing color of Goodwin's eyes from blue to red. It's only a few seconds, but to Sam, it seems like an hour.

"Normal? Normal? Why do you want to be normal? Anyone can be normal. You are special, Sam, and that is why I am here. I would not come here for a 'normal' kid. I came here for a special kid. I came here for you! I have seen you fight. I have seen you at the doctor's office getting your treatments. A normal kid would have given up by now.

"You are just like this acorn. You are full of potential. All you must do is believe in the acorn, but more importantly, believe in yourself. You see, Sam, you are much more powerful than you know. You are a special person who has a very special purpose. You have to unlock your mind to see the world differently.

"You can accomplish anything if you put a laser-like focus on it. Say these words with me. Say these words at the top of your lungs. Believe in these words, and you will see what I see. Speak these words: "I am strong. I am powerful. I am brave.""

After Goodwin speaks these words, he floats off the ground, and Sam can feel the emotion behind his words. The wind picks up, and the smell of lavender fills his nose. Sam thinks, "Is this real, or am I dreaming?"

Goodwin puts his hand on Sam's shoulder, sending warmth through his body. Sam can feel the power flowing through his body. He watches as Goodwin's eyes slowly turned from red to blue.

"Now it's your turn to say these words," says Goodwin.

Sam takes a deep breath and focuses all his energy on those words. Looking Goodwin directly in his eyes, he says, "I AM STRONG! I AM POWERFUL! I AM BRAVE!"

When Sam speaks the words, he feels pins and needles flow through his body. The wind picks up to a furious pace, and Goodwin has a big smile on his face. He put his fist out and asks Sam if he saw just a regular acorn now. Goodwin slowly opens his hand, and to Sam's amazement, the acorn has changed. It is no longer a normal acorn. It is now beautiful! The acorn looks as if it is vibrating, and now instead of its normal brown color, it is a beautiful array of all colors.

"What did you do to it?" Sam asks curiously.

Goodwin explains, "I didn't do anything to it—you did. You spoke those powerful words, and you believed in yourself. When you have this belief, you change the way you think, and everything around you will change. Remember to always believe in yourself and maximize your potential. This acorn is yours. Please keep it safe. It is the key to the Land of Aurora. It will open the door only if you believe."

"Where is the door?" Sam asks with excitement.

Goodwin takes a serious tone. "Before I show you the door, I need you to promise me that you will believe in yourself and do all you can to avoid being normal. You are so much more. Do you promise?"

"I promise," Sam says.

Goodwin pulls the acorn out of his pocket and says with a booming tone, "I AM STRONG! I AM POWERFUL! I AM BRAVE!" He then floats many feet into the air and spins. The clouds grow even darker, and Sam must hold on to a tree next to him so the wind does not knock him down. Goodwin throws the acorn into the stream. Sam is not prepared for what happens next.

A whirlpool forms in the stream. It looks like a lightning storm under the water. Suddenly, an oak tree grows out of the water. Goodwin speaks the words again, "I AM STRONG! I AM POWERFUL! I AM BRAVE!" He speaks with an even stronger voice than the last time. The tree shot up to over one hundred feet tall in a matter of seconds. Sam cannot believe what he is seeing.

"Do you believe you are special now, Sam?" Goodwin asks. Sam stands in silence. "Sam, you are the only one who can save my world. Will you help me?"

"Yes. What do I need to do?" Sam replies.

Goodwin explains, "I need you to open the door and travel to the Land of Aurora. When you get there—"

Just then, two large figures appear on the path. Goodwin turns to Sam quickly and says, "You must go now. Take your acorn and speak the magic words to open the door. When you get to the Land of Aurora, find the Gatekeeper. Tell her Goodwin sent you. Tell her they are here, and they have found you."

"Who found me?" Sam demands. "What's the Gatekeeper?"

Goodwin shouts at Sam. "There is no time! GO!"

Sam runs over to the grand oak tree.

Sam clutches the acorn to his chest and screams with authority, "I AM STRONG! I AM POWERFUL! I AM BRAVE!" Once the words are spoken, the tree vibrates, a crack forms at the base of the trunk, exposing a bright light. Pieces of the trunk peel off until a door is big enough for Sam to pass through. The branches of the tree bend toward the ground, gently hugging Sam into the portal. Sam can feel the power of the tree, pulling him into the Land of Aurora.

At that moment, Sam is distracted by two figures coming toward him. Goodwin holds them off for as long as he can, but the two figures are now at the tree. They shake the branches while screaming at Sam.

"Sam! You cannot go to Aurora! You are not special. You can't do these things," says a voice coming from the two figures.

Sam loses his concentration for just a minute and doubts himself. At that moment, the light dims, and Sam no longer feels calm. He is pulled into the portal, but instead of easily floating forward, he is spiraling out of control. He is on a collision course with the unknown.

Sam is spinning out of control within the portal for what seems to be an hour, until he finally sees something. At first, he cannot tell what it is, but then it comes into focus. It is a giant, dark ocean. Sam drops into the ocean and immediately swims to the top to get air. Sam is alone and very afraid

CHAPTER 4

THE *S.S. BRIELLE* & THE MEHLER ANCHOR

Sam is in the ocean with giant swelling waves. He struggles and uses all his might to stay afloat, but with each crashing wave, he doubts himself more. He is out of breath, his body is cramping, and he looks to the heavens and screams, "Help me! Please help me!" Sam is about to give up, but in the distance, he sees it. He sees what appears to be a great pirate ship heading in his direction. He digs deep within himself and says, "I will make it. I will survive. I am strong. I am powerful. I am brave."

Suddenly, Sam has reason to have hope. He is breathing easier, and the cramps leave his body. He treads water, watching the pirate ship get closer and closer until it is finally next to him.

When the ship is next to Sam, two interesting-looking men look at him. One says, "That's a bad place to be hanging out. Do you want to get on the ship?"

Sam looks bewildered. "Yes, please. I have been here for hours." The two men toss Sam a rope.

Sam holds on to the rope so tightly that his knuckles turn white. He can't wait to lie down and catch his breath. The two men pull Sam out of the water and into their boat. He is so grateful to be out of the ocean.

Sam immediately kisses the boat, looks at the two men and says, "Thank...thanks...thank you!" In shock, he realizes the two men are not men. They stand like they are human, but they have the head of a horse. These men are half man, half horse. They are horsemen! Sam stands in shock and silence. His silence speaks a thousand words.

One of the horsemen breaks the silence and says, "My name is Jamie, and this is Earl. We are the captains of this ship, the *S.S. Brielle*. Who are you?"

Sam, still frozen with fear, did not speak.

"Jamie, this one can't speak," says Earl. "I think we should throw him back."

"Ha ha. I think we will give him another chance. Then Jamie turns to Sam. "Boy, what is your name? How did you get here?" he asks in a stern voice.

"My...my name?" Sam asks, with a shaky voice.

"Yes, boy! What is your name?" Earl demands.

For a moment, Sam's mind is blank, and he cannot remember his name. Suddenly, something in his pocket vibrates. He remembers the acorn. Sam pulls it from his pocket and remembers what Goodwin had told him. He remembers that he is strong, powerful, and brave. He remembers he has potential. He stands up and looks at Jamie and Earl in the eyes and says, "My name is Sam. Goodwin sent me here."

Jamie and Earl stumble backward as their eyes opened wide.

"Jamie, do you think this is him?" Earl questions.

"I don't know, but we have waited a long time for this boy if it is him," Jamie replies. Turning his attention to Sam, he asks, "Sam, where are you from, and how did you get here?"

Sam finds the courage to explain. "I'm from Downingtown, Pennsylvania. I used this acorn to get here. I was told that I need to visit the Gatekeeper once I got here."

"Wow! It is him!" Earl shouts with excitement.

Earl and Jamie kneel on the ground and salute Sam. "We have waited for hundreds of years for your arrival. I cannot believe you are finally here! There is so much I need to tell you!" Jamie says all in one breath.

Sam asks, "Why are you waiting for me?"

"Jamie and I are part of the queen's Royal Guard. Our mission is to bring happiness, health, and peace to our people and to make a difference in this world. We begin every day with one goal in mind: use kindness to make someone's day brighter," Earl explains.

"That's great, but why do you need me?" Sam asks, not certain he is ready for the answer.

"Sam, there was a time when everyone was like us. The queen ruled the land, and everyday people would help each other, be kind to one another, living with peace and joy in our hearts. Everyone loved everyone else with so much passion that my heart and soul were filled with joy. Everything was perfect until the 'others' came." Earl seems sad as he speaks.

"The others?" Sam asks.

"Yes, the others," Earl replies. "I remember it like it was yesterday. Everyone was at the Town Square for our annual celebration of the Mighty Oak Tree. You see Sam, the Mighty Oak was a magic tree that represented life... It represented love... It represented growth and potential. It represented new beginnings. It was everything to us and our queen. It is a constant reminder of how we should live our lives. It reminded us to bring happiness to those around us. I remember dancing with my friends when I first heard it."

Earl lowers his head and holds his face. Sam could tell he was holding back tears and that the story was very difficult for him to share.

"There was a sound that was nothing compared to the feeling that took over my body when I saw them—the others." Earl's frightened tone has Sam's attention. "The sound was the thunderous steps of hundreds of men on horses running toward our town. With every step the horses took, I felt a darkness come over me. This was the first time I ever felt the sickness. When the men arrived in the square, everyone was frozen with fear and sadness. We have never felt those emotions before, so we didn't understand it."

Tears roll down Earl's face, which was Jamie's cue to take over the conversation. "The leader of these men is a man named Mr. C. Mr. C got off his horse and offered a cold dark stare to the queen and the Mighty Oak. He said, 'I now control you and this land.' The Mighty Oak began to shake and drop its leaves. Our reminder of how to be kind had gotten the sickness from Mr. C. The Mighty Oak began to crumble apart, but just before it crumbled to the ground, it produced four acorns as a sign of hope. That's where you come into play."

"Where I come into play?" Sam asks, puzzled.

"Yes, you. Do you have it?" asks Earl.

"Have what?" Questions Sam.

"The acorn..." Earl replies.

Sam reaches into his pocket and pulls the acorn out.

"There is a prophecy that says once the special child from another world comes with his army, that is when the darkness and sickness will leave this land. After the darkness leaves the land, we are to plant the four acorns together. When the acorns are planted, the Mighty Oak will return. Sam, you have one of the four acorns," Jamie explains eagerly.

Sam asks, "Who has the other three acorns?"

Earl answers quickly, "Goodwin has one, the Gatekeeper has one, and our queen has one."

"When I was with Goodwin, he told me that I need to find the Gatekeeper," Sam says to Jamie and Earl.

"We are headed east to see the queen. The Gatekeeper is to the west of us. If Mr. C. knows that you are here, we must move quickly. Earl, prepare the lifeboat for Sam," Jamie commands.

Earl runs to the back of the ship and packs a bag for Sam. He preps the boat and gets everything ready.

"Sam, you must hurry. The boat is ready. I packed some food and water for you, and I have a special gift for you," Earl says. He reaches into his pocket and pulls out an anchor about an inch long. With a giant grin on his face, he hands it to Sam.

"What am I supposed to do with this?" Sam asks.

"It's an anchor for your boat. It's very special, so please keep it safe," Earl explains.

"How is that tiny anchor going to help steady my boat?" Sam questions.

"Sam, this is the one-of-a-kind Mehler Anchor. This anchor represents strength. It is strong enough to hold your boat in place during the biggest storms with the mightiest of waves. More importantly, it is meant to give you strength in your darkest times or when you are scared. When you are scared, hold this anchor in your hand, close your eyes, and say, 'I AM BRAVE!' When you do this, visualize the fear leaving your body. This anchor will give you strength and keep you grounded."

Sam gets in the boat, and Jamie and Earl lower it into the ocean. As the two boats drift apart, the new friends wave goodbye. As Sam watches the *S.S. Brielle* go out of sight, he prepares his boat for the journey to the west. He raises the sail on his small boat and is ready to go, but there is one problem. There is no wind! Sam knows the wind will come eventually, so he eats his dinner and waits for the wind to come. As Sam is enjoying his dinner, he watches the sun set and the stars come out.

Sam is amazed by the number of stars that he can see. He has never seen so many stars before. The sea is calm, and there is still no wind, but Sam is at peace. He thinks about how far he has come since he met Goodwin. He thinks about how much his mother and father love him. He thinks about how hard all his doctors have worked to make him better. He thinks about how much his friends and people in his community have done for him. Finally, he thinks about how great it is to be a special kid. Sam sits with his thoughts as he gazes at the beauty of the stars and drifts off to sleep.

CHAPTER 5

THE SAIL, THE WIND & THE BELIEF STONE

Kersplash! Kersplash!

Sam awakes to a splash of water on his face. It is morning, and his eyes adjust to the light. As Sam's eyes adjust, he sees where the splash is coming from. He sees a pod of the biggest whales he has ever seen. These are not like any ordinary whales. They are twice the size of blue whales and have a row of spikes down their backs. Each spike of the whale is bigger than the boat Sam is in. One whale gets so close to the boat that Sam can touch it. The whale's deep-purple eyes are about five feet high and five feet wide. Every time a whale gets close to the boat, Sam feels it staring at him. The whales finally swim away, and Sam turns his attention to the boat's sail. He begins his journey for the day.

Looking at his sail, he is saddened to see it is still flat, and there is no wind. He eats his breakfast and waits. And waits. And waits.

At mid-afternoon, there is still no wind. The temperature is over one hundred degrees, and there is no shelter from the intense heat and sunlight. Sam swallows the last of his water and eats the last of his food. He is afraid, and he feels lost and alone. He cries, as his thoughts tell him that he won't make it off the boat. He feels he is going to be stranded forever. He is sad because he does not want to let everyone down. At this moment, Sam is losing all hope. Then something magical happens!

Something in Sam's pocket vibrates, and Sam reaches in to grab it. This time it was not the acorn, but the Mehler Anchor. As Sam places the Mehler Anchor in his hand, he remembers what Earl said. *This anchor will give you strength in your darkest times. When you are scared, hold this anchor in your hand and say, "I am brave."* Sam remembers his new friend's caring tone, and squeezes the anchor in his hand. He closes his eyes and shouts at the top of his lungs, "I AM BRAVE!" Immediately, he feels a wave of calm come over him, and he slowly opens his eyes.

Sam looks out at the ocean. He spots two blurry figures moving fast on the water. The only thing he can make out is the water flying up after the figures go by him. He watches in awe for a few moments, trying to make sense of it. He hears someone say, "Hey, handsome, what are you doing?"

Sam is startled. He jumps backward, tripping over his own feet. "Who are you?" Sam asks.

"My name is K-Harp, and that is Sarge," she says as she points to the splashes on the water. "Sarge, it's okay. We found him!"

Just then, another person appears on the boat. "Hello, I'm Sarge."

Sam gulps. "Hello."

K-Harp and Sarge are beautiful creatures. They seem to be a hybrid of a human and cheetah, with average height and beautiful eyes. They have human bodies but are covered in fur resembling a cheetah.

"I can't believe it's you!" Sarge exclaims. "When Jamie and Earl told us you were here, we had to see it for ourselves.

"Are you on your way to see the Gatekeeper?" K-Harp asks.

"I am," Sam replies. "But I am waiting for the wind to pick up. I have been here all day, but there is no wind," Sam explains with frustration.

"I thought they said you were the one. The special child who would save our world," Sarge says, seeming a little confused.

K-Harp speaks up. "He is the one, Sarge, but he doesn't believe yet."

"Believe? Believe in what?" Sam asks.

Sarge and K-Harp have huge grins on their faces after hearing Sam's question. "Believe in yourself, silly!" Sam gazes at the bottom of the boat, with his head held low.

"Pick your head up and listen to what I have to say!" says K-Harp with enthusiasm. Sam looks right into K-Harp's eyes. "Sam, you have a choice. Be the wind or be the sail. Which one do you want to be?"

Sam is surprised and confused by the question. He looks blankly at K-Harp and says, "I don't understand."

K-Harp explains, "In your life, you have the choice to be the wind or the sail. If you choose to be the sail, you must wait for the wind to fill your sail to decide where you want to go. If you are the wind, you choose the direction and will have control over your life. Now Sam, do you want to be the wind or the sail?"

"I want to be in control of my life. I choose the wind," Sam says thoughtfully.

"Sam, remember this when you go back to your world. In your life, if you choose to be the sail and let others tell you how to live your life, you will always have to travel in their direction. If you choose to be the wind, you will make life happen to you and achieve great things! Be the wind, not the sail. In our world, being the wind versus the sail is quite literal. If you truly are the chosen one, then you can control the wind," K-Harp explains.

"How can I control the wind?" Sam questions.

"With a little bit of help and a whole lot of belief," Sarge said wisely. She reaches into her pocket and pulls out a beautiful purple stone. "This is a Belief Stone," she explains to Sam. "They are very rare. Legend has it, that when the chosen one comes to this land, he or she can use this stone to control the elements. For it to work, the chosen one must fully believe in himself."

She hands the stone to Sam. He holds the stone and closes his fist around it. He looks into Sarge's eyes and says with excitement, "I know what to do with this!"

Standing tall with the stone in his hand, Sam closes his eyes, mustering his inner strength and belief in himself. He draws a deep breath in and shouts, "I BELIEVE!" Just then, the clouds move and block the sun. A huge thunderstorm moves in. A huge gust of wind fills Sam's sail, and his boat sails westward.

Sam opens his eyes. For the first time, he knows he is special. He knows he is the one. He turns to K-Harp and Sarge, but they are gone. He can see them off in the distance, heading east.

CHAPTER 6

THE QUEEN & THE BAKER

Meanwhile, on the *S.S. Brielle*, Earl is having trouble navigating through the fog. "I can't see anything, but I know we are close to the shore." As the boat approaches the shore, they can see what seems to be a bright light in the fog.

"This isn't fog, Earl," Jamie said. "This is smoke. The town is on fire! We need to move fast and find the queen!" Earl quickly drops two more sails on the *S.S. Brielle*, increasing its speed. The *Brielle* races full speed into the harbor, crashing through the docks, then grounds itself on the shore. Jamie and Earl get their swords, jump from the boat, and run for Town Square.

"Earl, there are too many soldiers here. We can't defeat them all. We need to stay in the shadows and use the underground tunnels," Jamie explains, referring to the series of underground tunnels long forgotten. Only the queen and the Royal Guard knows they exist. They are being used as secret tunnels now, helping the queen to move about the town undetected.

Earl and Jamie carefully sneak into the closest tunnel entrance. The entrance is about one thousand feet away, under Karen's Bakery. Jamie and Earl find their way to the back of the bakery, then climb through the window. The roof is on fire, and the bakery is filling with smoke.

"Earl, we have to make it to the tunnel entrance. Everyone and everything depend on us. Get low to the ground and follow me," Jamie says.

Jamie and Earl are almost to the secret entrance, but the fire is growing. Part of the ceiling is collapsing. Flames climb the walls and cover part of the floor. Jamie and Earl make it to the secret door. Slowly, Jamie opens the door. He crawls in first, followed by Earl. Just as Earl closes the hatch behind him, the roof collapses, coming down with a loud *boom*. The impact of the roof hitting the hatch sends Earl flying off the ladder, plummeting ten feet. He lands right on top of Jamie.

"Earl! Would you mind getting off me?" Jamie shouts.

"Ugh... Ouch! That hurt. Sorry, Jamie," Earl replies.

"Why did you fall on me?" Jamie seems annoyed.

"I haven't practiced falling enough," Earl says with a chuckle.

Earl and Jamie head down the tunnel. After a few minutes, they hear people talking. They turn the corner and see the queen with her most trusted of the Royal Guard. They look defeated. They sit on the ground, covered in black soot from the fires.

The queen is one of the most beautiful creatures in the land. She has long dark hair and emerald-green eyes. She stands at about six feet tall and always has a smile on her face. Even in the darkest of times, she keeps her positive attitude, but today, she is different.

Jamie and Earl kneel before the queen. "Your Majesty, we have found him. We have found the one!" says Jamie.

"The one is here? How long has he been here?" the queen asks with excitement.

Jamie explains to the queen. "He has already met Goodwin and received his acorn. He has received the Belief Stone from K-Harp and Sarge, and we have given him the Mehler Anchor. The only thing left is the Promise Stone. We need to move as soon as possible to the *S.S. Brielle*. We will head west and find the one. He is on his way to meet the Gatekeeper."

"I am sorry, Jamie and Earl," the queen says in despair. "All hope has been lost. I have been defeated. We are broken. Mr. C. has destroyed our lands, broken our families, changed our friendships, and taken over our kingdom. We are just going to wait in this dark place. We will wait for the end. Mr. C is too powerful and has wiped out our resources. Jamie and Earl, what is the point of moving forward?"

Jamie and Earl have a look of shock and sadness on their faces. They lower their heads. With tears streaming down Jamie's face, he looks at the queen and says, "Your Majesty, it has been a great run. It has been an honor to serve in your Royal Guard. We were just too late. I wish we could go back in time before Mr. C. came to our land. Everything is different now."

At that moment, Karen, the baker, stands up and says, "I can't believe what I'm hearing. Mr. C. has taken nearly everything from me. I have lost friends, I have lost my family, and my bakery no longer exists. There is nothing left. Mr. C. has destroyed more of me than any of you, but I will not let him win!
The only way Mr. C. can truly win is if we all give up. These are the darkest times of our lives, but we have the choice of how we want to live. The one is here, and he needs us to remember. All of us will die one day, but how many of us ever truly live?" the baker says. Your Majesty, the one is here, and he needs you to remember who you are and the promise you made to us."

Just then, a bright light comes from the queen's dress pocket. The bright light has a warmth to its glow. The queen reaches into her pocket and pulls something out. She holds it in her hand and then falls to her knees. "I do remember the promise that I made to all of you. I promised to be here for you and make a difference in this world. I promised to fight for you to ensure everyone's life made a difference. I understand now. I apologize for letting the darkness of Mr. C. control who I was. Thank you, Karen, for showing me the light.

The queen stands up and looks directly into Jamie's eyes. "It is time. Ready the ship. Mr. C. may have burned our land and caused us pain, but he can never take away our hope. We are the only ones who can
decide if we will keep fighting. I choose to fight until my last breath. I am your queen, and we have a child that needs our help. Who is with me?"

Everyone stands up, dusts themselves off, and in unison they say, "I am with you! I will fight!"

"What are we waiting for?" shouts Earl. "Let's go!"

The queen and her Royal Guard leave for the *S.S. Brielle*. After a quick run through the tunnels, the group finds an exit point near the *S.S. Brielle*.

CHAPTER 7

THE *S.S. BRIELLE* WILL SAIL AGAIN

The queen and the Royal Guard emerge from the tunnel and see that the S.S. Brielle has been grounded and their city is engulfed in flames. She looks at Earl and asks, "Is the *S.S. Brielle* able to float?"

With a sense of pride, Earl replies, "Your Majesty, the *S.S. Brielle* may be a young boat, but she has been through more storms than any vessel in your fleet. She has a spirit that cannot be broken. She will most definitely float."

The queen turns to look at her city again. Her faith starts to waver. "My beautiful city!" cries the queen. "Why would this happen? Why would this happen to me?" she says to herself. "I must not, I will not lose my faith again! I made a promise, and I will keep it."

Looking at Jamie and Earl, the queen commands, "Jamie and Earl, get the *S.S. Brielle* ready to sail!" She turns to the rest of the Royal Guard and calls each one by their name. "Laura, Joe, Sandy, Steph, Kat, Michelle, Ken, Tammy, Amanda, Andrea, Amy, Jen, Glen, Jackie, Matt, Sheryl, Ed, Blake, Beck, Shannon, Rob, Bob, Carol, and Patti, will you help to push the *Brielle* back into the water?"

The queen and the Royal Guard line up against the S.S. *Brielle*, and the queen says, "Okay, on the count of three, we push. One, two, three, PUSH! One, two, three, PUSH! One, two, three, PUSH!"

The S.S. *Brielle* is moving very little on each push. Exhausted by their efforts, they realize they still have a long way to go. Blake, one of the youngest members of the Royal Guard, remarks, "We need just a little more strength to get the boat back in the water. I don't know if we have enough strength to do that."

The queen answers, "I made you a promise. Our only option is to get this boat into the water. Everyone must keep their faith. Now, one, two, three, PUSH! One, two, three, PUSH! One, two, three, PUSH!"

Everyone is giving it all they have, but the S. S. Brielle is barely moving. The queen puts her hand in her pocket and says aloud, "I believe, and I made a promise! The *Brielle* will sail again!"

Just as she spoke, Earl shouts as he points toward the water. "Here they come! YES! They are here!"

The queen and the Royal Guard walk around the *S.S. Brielle* to see what Earl is talking about. Only about a mile out, K-Harp and Sarge are coming toward them, but they are not alone. They have the rest of the Speedsters with them.

They arrive at the *Brielle*, and K-Harp says to the queen, "Sam is here! The special child is here! We must get you to him as soon as possible. How can we help?"

The queen gives K-Harp a huge hug. "We need to get the *Brielle* into the water," the queen says. Sarge jumps onto the *Brielle* and grabs the rope. She ties it to the giant hook in the front of the boat, then drops the rope to the ground.

K-Harp organizes the process. "Speedsters to front of the boat, and grab the rope!" She turns to the queen. "Your Majesty, please do a countdown and push while we pull."

The queen announces, "One, two, three, PUSH!" She is pleased to see the Royal Guard and the Speedsters working together as a team to get the *S.S. Brielle* back into the water. They focus on their mission and believe in themselves. The *Brielle* moved inch by inch toward the breaking surf. With a joint effort, the *S.S. Brielle* is now back in the water.

Jamie lowers the ladder and says, "Everyone hurry and get in the boat!"

The Royal Guard, the queen, and the Speedsters all climb the ladder to the boat. Jamie calls out, "We are setting sail and heading to the Gatekeeper. We must get there quickly because we are running out of time." The sails are dropped, and off they go, but the speed is slow.

K-Harp looks at Sarge and asks, "Are you thinking what I'm thinking?"

Sarge smiles as she speaks. "Yeah, I think we need a turbo."

K-Harp runs to the front of the boat, calling the Speedsters. She shouts to the group, "Take the rope and follow me. It's time to kick in the turbo!"

K-Harp, Sarge, and the Speedsters grab the rope and jump from the front of the boat. They run on top of the water as fast as they can. Together, they have the strength and are so fast that they are pulling the boat. The speed increases tenfold. Everything is falling into place, and they see the Gatekeeper soon.

CHAPTER 8

THE GATEKEEPER & HALL OF MIRRORS

Meanwhile, Sam spots the island where the Gatekeeper lives, a tropical island with a volcano. Sam docks his boat in the island harbor and gets out of the boat. There is not much on this island other than the docks and a giant staircase that ascends the mountain past the clouds. Sam looks closely at the staircase, and he knows what he must do. He starts his way up that staircase. The climb is exhausting. He has been moving for over two hours to reach the top of the staircase. He knows he must get there.

The top of the staircase is covered with tropical flowers. There is a huge door with a giant knocker and a carving of a giant eyeball. Sam walks up to the door, takes the giant knocker, and knocks three times. The last knock on the door gives a loud *boom*. Every bird on the island flees from the sound, abandoning their hiding spots. Sam looks down on the island from the top of the staircase and hears a voice.

"Who is there?" the voice asks. Sam looks around but sees no one. He realizes the voice is coming from behind the huge door. Again, the voice asks, "Who is there?" This time more loudly and with authority. Sam looks at the door and says boldly, "I am Sam."

"We have been waiting for you," the voice responds. "Are you ready to see yourself?"

Sam is a little confused by this question. He answers, "I guess so."

In an angry tone, the voice responds, "You guess? You *guess*? I asked you a question! Sam, are you ready to see yourself?"

Sam pauses, then says, "Yes. Yes, I am ready to see myself."

The eye on the door opens, and the lock retracts. Sam cautiously pulls the door open and walks inside.

As Sam walks in, he is greeted by two people, a man and a woman. The woman approaches Sam and introduces herself.

"Hello, Sam, my name is Colleen, and this is Jeff. Welcome to the Hall of Mirrors. In this hall, you will take your final test. When you pass this test,

you will meet the Gatekeeper. Many have taken this test, but only the true of heart will pass. He who passes may leave the island."

Sam looks at Colleen and asks, "What do you mean when you say, 'may leave the island'?"

Jeff responds, "It's a huge reward to be able to meet the Gatekeeper and still be able to travel back to your land. With huge rewards come huge consequences. If you do not pass this test, you will become part of the island. Do you wish to take the test?"

Sam is excited about the opportunity to meet the Gatekeeper, but the fear of the possibility of being stuck on the island weighs on him. He doubts himself and thinks of all the reasons he will fail.

As Sam ponders his role, the acorn, Mehler Anchor, and Belief Stone ring and vibrate in his pocket. He reaches for them and shows the vibrance of his tokens.

Colleen is mesmerized. She looks at Sam and says, "You have three of the four artifacts. You are the one! You cannot doubt yourself with this test. Speak with confidence and believe in yourself."

"I'm scared, and I don't know what will happen if I don't pass this test," Sam says.

"It is okay and normal to be afraid," Colleen responds. "True courage cannot happen without fear. Everyone is afraid, but only the brave have courage. The fact that you made it this far means that you are brave. The thing that you will need to pass this test is positive self-talk and powerful words. I will help you before you take the test."

Colleen looks at Sam. "To be one with yourself, to be a true believer, you must change the way you think and the way you speak. Sam, you must understand our lives are what our thoughts make of it. We are who we think we are. We become what we imagine about ourselves. Everyone has the gift of choice, but very few use it correctly. To change your life, you must change your thoughts, so you must change your words. There are words we use every day that render us powerless. Little by little these words have the power to take away our strength and purpose," Coleen says. "Sam, to pass your next test, you will need to eliminate certain words from your vocabulary.

"The first word to eliminate is the word *try*. When we say we will 'give it a try,' or 'I will try to do that,' we are not committed to doing it. This word gives you an easy way out. You must commit to your thoughts and words. There is no more *try*. It is either *I will* or *I will not*.

"Other similar words that take your power away are 'maybe,' 'I guess,' 'I hope so,' 'I wish,' and 'I need to.' There is no 'maybe,' or 'I guess.' It is either 'I know,' or 'I don't know.' Change the phrases 'I hope so' or 'I wish' to 'I know so, and I will.'

"I am sure you have said, 'I hope I will get better,' or 'I wish I were healthy,' or 'I need to get better,' or even, 'I *have* to get better.' Hoping and wishing are not strategies. You need to show commitment. Change your words. Change your thoughts. Say, 'I WILL GET BETTER,' and believe it with all of your heart. Say it out loud. Sam, say, 'I am healthy!'"

And with that, Sam screams with authority, "I am healthy!"

"The most important word that takes your power away is the word *can't*. This word has no place in your brain—it is the killer of dreams. Sam, you can do whatever you imagine. You can be whoever you choose to be.

You only must believe it. Look how far you have come. Look how many people told you that you would not get here, that you could not be the one. Sam, you are a special child who can accomplish anything. Please trust yourself, and become the one you were meant to be. Are you ready for the test?"

Sam takes a deep breath and looks at Colleen in the eyes and speaks with authority. "I am ready!"

Colleen walks across the room and opens the door. "Okay, Sam, it is time. Please walk this way."

Sam follows her through the door. He walks into a dark room and hears the sweetest voice.

"Let the test begin! Find your true self, Sam."

With that, the room lights up and seven mirrors surround Sam. He can see an infinite amount of self-reflection.

The room goes pitch-black. Sam hears a voice. "Who are you?" The light returns, and Sam sees an older version of himself in the mirrors. He studies himself, and he looks to be in his early thirties, wearing a captain's uniform, with his head held high. He hears the voice. "Is this you, Sam?" Sam stands in silence as he studies what is before him. The lights go dim once again.

The voice asks, "Who are you, Sam?" Sam sees himself again in the mirror, but at his current age. He is playing soccer with his friends, and he is the fastest kid on the team. His health is not keeping him down. He finally sees himself as a normal kid. The lights dim again, and Sam hears the voice ask, "How could this be you? You are sick. You can't be the fastest kid on the team."

Sam feels familiar doubt, and the lights suddenly come back on. This time, the picture he sees in the mirror is himself in a hospital bed. He has lost all his hair, and his eyes are faded. Sam can feel the sadness and despair. Next to Sam, in anguish, is his mother, her eyes filled with sadness. The reflection of his mother asks Sam, "Who are you?" Tears roll down her face. Again, the room goes dark. Sam is obviously upset.

"I'm sorry, Mom. I love you."

The lights grow bright again, but this time there is no reflection. The mirror is empty. Sam hears the voice again. "Sam, you can decide who you want to be, but you must choose your true, authentic self. Everything that has happened to you in your life has made you who you are; however, those things do not define you. Sam, it's time for you to decide who you are."

With that, the lights again grow dim. Sam sits in the dark with his thoughts. He remembers his struggle with his sickness. He remembers the love of his family, and relishes in how far he has come in his journey. He thinks about all the forces that depend on him, and he thinks about his home and what he must do.

All of a sudden the Mehler Anchor starts to vibrate in his pocket, and Sam starts to understand who he really is.

Sam sees his reflection in the mirror. There are no tricks or visions this time. It is the reflection he recognizes. The voice comes back and says, "Who are you, Sam?"

Sam takes a deep breath and looks into his own eyes in his reflection and says, "I am Sam. I am powerful. I am courageous. I am kind. I am special. I have a disease, but that disease does not define me. I bring joy to those around me because I choose to be happy. I am at peace with myself because I know who I am. I love who I am!"

The lights go off, and Sam stands there and understands who he is and what his purpose is.

Sam hears a voice. "Well done, Sam."

CHAPTER 9

THE VOYAGE HOME & THE PROMISE STONE

The room is once again dark; the smell of lavender fills the room. Just then, the floor opens. Sam floats down and descends, but not in fear, in peace. As he gets closer to the ground, he can see someone there. When he finally reaches the bottom, he can make out the figure he sees standing in front of him. It is the most beautiful woman he has ever seen—her lovely blond hair, emerald-green eyes, with an aura of love, happiness, and peace.

"Hello, Sam, my name is Melissa. I am the Gatekeeper. You have traveled a long distance to find me. I am very happy that you have discovered your true self and you passed the final test!" Melissa reminds Sam, "Always remember who you are. You still have a huge journey ahead of you, and it won't be easy. It will be what you make it. I permit you to travel between my world and yours. You have another artifact to collect before you move on. Your friends and the queen are right outside, waiting to help you get home."

The Gatekeeper points to the door. Sam looks and turns back to ask the Gatekeeper a question, only to find she is gone. Sam walks to the door, opens it, and walks out.

Sam emerges from the Hall of Mirrors, slightly blinded by the light. His eyes slowly adjust, and he sees the *S.S. Brielle* docking in the harbor. He takes off, running for the ship. When he reaches the ship, the first person he runs into is Earl. As Earl ties the boat to the dock, he notices Sam.

"Sam, the queen is here to meet you. Have you visited with the Gatekeeper?" Earl asks.

"Yes! And I passed the test! The Gatekeeper permitted me to pass between worlds!" Sam explains with excitement.

Just then, the queen emerges from the ship and descends to the dock. Sam approaches her and takes a knee. "Your Majesty, I am ready for my journey."

"Rise, my son," the queen says as she extends her hand. "You have passed every test in your world and my world. Everything you have done has led you to this place. There is only one lesson left for you before your journey back to your world."

The queen reaches into her pocket and pulls out the Promise Stone. "Sam, this is the last item you will need to make your journey home. This Promise Stone will work only with someone who has a true heart."

The queen holds the stone and asks Sam to take it. He reaches out and clasps the stone. The queen then reaches out and embraces Sam's hand.

"Sam, look at me," says the queen. Sam is drawn into her emerald eyes. "To achieve anything great in this world, you must make a promise to yourself and keep it. Anyone who has an impact on this world, on your world, or any world began with a promise to do something great. Do you promise to believe in yourself and save our world from Mr. C?"

Sam looks at the queen. With conviction, he replies, "My Queen, I promise."

"You are ready, Sam," says the queen. "Place the Promise Stone with the Mehler Anchor, Belief Stone, and the Acorn."

Sam holds all the items in his hand and grasps them tightly in his fist. He can feel them vibrate as a bright-blue light shines from his hand. The light and vibration suddenly stop. Sam opens his hand. To his surprise, his hand holds only the acorn. "Where did they go?" Sam asks the queen.

The queen smiles brightly and says, "The acorn has always been the key to travel between our worlds. The Promise Stone, Mehler Anchor, and the Belief Stone have been absorbed into the acorn and will come back to you when you need them."

"Do you remember what Goodwin told you about the acorn?"

Sam remembers. "Yes, from this tiny acorn, mighty oaks will grow."

"That is correct, Sam," says the queen. "There is another part of your lesson. This one acorn will turn into a mighty oak tree, then produce thousands of acorns that possess the same magic. Sam, you are the Mighty Oak. We need you to go back to your world and find believers like you. Bring them here. Only an army of believers can beat Mr. C." The queen holds Sam's attention. "Remember everything you have learned here, always keep your faith in yourself." The queen explains, "You are special. We need other special kids like yourself. Will you do this for me?" she asks.

"Yes," Sam replies, confident in his words.

"Are you ready to go home, Sam?" He nods. "Then hold the acorn in your hand and ask it to take you home."

Sam closes his eyes, focuses on the queen's words, and says, "Take me home."

The acorn vibrates, and Sam begins to float off the ground, but he is not afraid. "Take me home, Acorn!" he screams. He feels a jolt through his body and senses the familiar smell of lavender. When he opens his eyes, he is back on the running path, where he first met Goodwin. Sam looks around with wonder and sees a red cape on the ground and thinks, "Am I really home?"

Just then, Sam hears his name called. He looks up in the distance and sees his mother. He quickly stuffs the red cape under his shirt and runs to her, calling out, "MOM! MOM! MOM!" When he reaches her, he gives her a huge hug, never wanting to let go.

His mom looks at him and says, "I was worried about you! I've been looking for you for an hour!"

"Only an hour?" Sam wonders.

"Lunch is ready," Sam's mom says.

He takes his mother's hand and walks back to their house. Sam looks back at the oak tree and whispers, "I will keep my promise. You will have your army soon."

Will you be a part of Sam's Army?

To be continued....

DEDICATION

Thanks to everyone who inspired me to write this book. I have watched so many of my loved ones struggle with cancer and other diseases. Through their struggles, they showed me true strength and how to live life to the fullest. I am truly blessed that they are part of my life.

To my beautiful wife, Melissa, (Gatekeeper), Joe, Marley, and CC – Thank you for being my rock and supporting me.

To Kim Mehler (Mehler Anchor) – Thank you for teaching me about friendship and strength. You are a beautiful mother, wife, and friend. We will see each other again.

To Brielle (*S.S. Brielle*) – You were the strongest most loving kid that I have ever met. You made more impact in your six years of life than most people do in a hundred years.

To Karen (baker) – Thank you for inspiring a movement. You have changed so many people's lives.

To Mark (Goodwin) – Thanks for being a friend and making the world a better place. You are an inspiration and a true leader.

To Jamie, Earl, Kristy, and Cari (Jamie, Earl, K-Harp, and Sarge) – Your laughter and charity inspired me to be a better human. You truly represent the mighty acorn.

To Christine (queen) – The charity group you started has changed so many lives. You have made the world a better place because of your actions. No time to slow down! Keep making the world a better place!

To Jeff and Colleen (from the Hall of Mirrors) – Thank you for keeping me grounded and pushing me to do things that I did not think were possible.

To Blake (the queen's Royal Guard) – You inspired me to write this book because I could not find a book that would give you strength during your surgery. Every book I found was depressing, so I wrote one for myself. This book is for you, kid.

To the rest of the Sam's Army – You know who you are and why you are in the Sam's Army. Continue to make this world a better place. What you do MATTERS!

To order another book, Power Cape, Power Pouch, or to donate a book to a children's hospital, please visit:
www.voyagetobravery.com.

My Vision and Promise to Sam and His Army

I wrote this story as a form of therapy for myself. One of my dear friends had just lost her battle with cancer, and my cousin's child was getting ready for brain surgery. I searched the bookstores and the internet for a book that would prepare this child for the upcoming surgery. To my dismay, there was not one book that would inspire him and provide courage to him. After that, I knew I had to write something that would provide children with the encouragement and self-empowerment they need to fight whatever battle they may be facing.

My Vision – I envisioned what a hospitalized child might be going through. They are sick, and their parents are going through one of the most challenging things a parent could go through. When looking for a book on the subject, every book I found described what the illness was, and it was depressing and powerless. My vision is to empower children and get them to focus on being healthy and positive. I see a scared child holding the Mehler Anchor to find their courage. I see that same child wearing the Power Cape to find their strength and power. I see parents playing "Sam's Army" with their child. I see strong, powerful, and brave children who believe in their ability to fight the things that scare them the most.

My Promise – My promise to you, and all of Sam's Army, is to provide this book to any children's hospital that is willing to accept it. I will do this with some of the profits of this book and from the donations made on my website. If we work together, we can provide some healing light into this world. Please consider donating, and I promise to continue to send out this message to as many children as I can reach. Thank you!

Your Friend,
Jeremiah Shelton

Author Bio

Jeremiah Shelton is one of the top motivational and leadership trainers in the automotive business. He works with adults, but his passion is to change the lives of children so that they become powerful adults.

Jeremiah Shelton grew up in Charlotte, North Carolina, and moved to West Chester, Pennsylvania, when he was eighteen years old. Jeremiah married his high school sweetheart at the age of twenty-three. Jeremiah and Melissa have three children, Joseph, Marley, and Cecilia.

At nineteen Jeremiah was trained and went to work for a Philadelphia Ford dealership as a finance and insurance manager. This is where he learned the retail lessons he would carry with him for the rest of his career. Since that time, Jeremiah became a district manager, regional manager, trainer, head of training, vice president, and partner of Strategic Diversified. Jeremiah is best known by his peers for his unique ability to teach adults, assist them in making real changes in their behavior, and ultimately making a positive impact on their lives.

Jeremiah has won many national awards for his contributions to his industry. He has won three all-star awards, two contender awards, and was the North American top producer and winner of the MVP award in 2019 from a major insurance company in the industry.

He is involved with many charities in his local area. The one dearest to his heart focuses on the people in his community that have been impacted by cancer. This charity group is made up of a bunch of runners and walkers whose mission is to help people and let cancer patients know that they are not alone. With this group, Jeremiah has run two Broad Street ten-mile runs and two half-marathons.

Jeremiah starts every day with the same mission: Do something every day that makes someone's life better.

Visit www.voyagetobravery.com for more information